REMEMBER, NO MATTER WHAT;

Miranda Oh

Couronne Publishing
WINNIPEG, MANITOBA

Miranda Oh
www.ohmirandaoh.com.com

Couronne Publishing
info@couronnepublishing.com
www.couronnepublishing.com

Cover design by Vanessa Mendozi
Images used under license Shutterstock.com

Ordering Information:
Quantity sales. Special discounts are available on quantity purchases by corporations, associations, and others. For details, contact the "Special Sales Department" at the address above.

Remember, No Matter what; Chin up, Tits Out- Miranda Oh.

1st edition
ISBN 978-0-9948637-1-3

This book is dedicated to H.M.M. Without their determination and ability to love fearlessly, this book would have never become a reality.

I woke up one morning to some noise outside our tent, and Riaan's arms wrapped tightly around me. I didn't really want to move much, but at the same time I didn't want someone stealing all of our stuff. So I grabbed my camera and turned it on. If someone was going to kill me, or kidnap me I wanted to leave photographic evidence of whom it was.

I slowly unzipped the tent, and stuck my camera outside in the direction of where I thought I heard the noise coming from. I started to snap photos and then I retracted my arm to review the photos I took.

Monkeys elbow deep in our cooler of food.

PROLOGUE

The pounding in my chest is deafening. I can't hear my thoughts over the thumping deep within my chest that feels like it's in my head. I lift my head and stare at the stranger in the mirror gawking back at me.

What the hell are you doing?

I twist up my bright red lipstick willing my hands to stop trembling. Putting lipstick on when you have nervous shaky hands is damn near impossible, especially bright red lipstick. Dropping it, I grasp the edge of the countertop breathing rapidly. I opened my eyes and stared at myself again then picked up the lipstick with still shaky hands.

Why did I choose to wear this color, dammit!

It shouldn't take a grown ass woman 5 minutes to put lipstick on!

After a couple of tries, I got the lipstick on. I stood up tall, my mum's voice in my head saying, "Chin up, tits out Hadley, exude confidence."

Confidence, what is that again?

It took me a whopping five hours to get ready for the evening, and no I wasn't going to an awards ceremony. I was simply going out for supper, nothing fancy, and nothing new.

Once I was a little satisfied with the way I looked, I strutted down the steps to show my parents.

"How do I look?" I asked as I spun around in a slow circle, the peplum of my dress fanning out a little.

"Too much?"

"Aww, you look great!" they both said, almost in unison. It was nauseating, I could feel the bile crawl up my esophagus, and then the tears start to well up in my eyes.

No. Please, not now.

I could immediately feel my chest start to close up, my breathing quickening, tears starting to trickle down my heavily made up face. BOOM, full blown panic attack.

Dammit, not again.

My parents shoot up from their couch, concerned, and overly worried.

Don't do that, please. It makes it worse.

"You okay Hadley?" My mum asked.

All I could muster in between my short gasps for air was, "Please leave. Please leave the house now! Before he comes." I continue to choke on the air, I felt like I was dying.

Yup, definitely dying. I can't do this. I can't do dinner. I'd rather die right now than go out for supper.

"What?" My dad pipes up, a little perturbed about my request.

I could only imagine what they're thinking right now. Their adult daughter, acting like a crazy person because she is too unstable to go out on a date with a new guy. Poor girl, they must be thinking. The thought of being pitied infuriated me.

"Please leave NOW! Before he comes, he is on his way. Please just GO! Anywhere but here!"

"Sam, grab the keys, let's go to Baba & Gigi's for a cup of tea." My mum calmly says as she walks to the kitchen and starts to dig through the cupboards.

"Why? What is the problem here?" My dad asks

"Sam, now. Grab the keys"

Please just gooooo!" I whined.

My poor dad, he is such a patient guy. He just doesn't get the mind of an unstable woman right now. I wish he didn't have to. As they leave the room to collect their things, I find myself a chair to sit on and stare at the black screen of my phone, waiting. Waiting for my breathing to go back to normal, or just flop over and die.

Both are totally possible at the moment.

My mum hands me a paper bag. "Here, breathe into this darling. It will help calm you down." Then she gave me that mum look. You know that look, the ones that only mums can give. They look deep into your soul, and give you that second of peace. They tell you everything is going to be all right, and that you are okay.

Fuck that look mummy, you don't know shit! You're happily married, a picture perfect magazine family, two somewhat healthy children, an amazing husband you actually love, and still like to be around, a big beautiful house, and a great successful business you built from the ground up. How do you know everything in my life will be okay?

I turn away from her somewhat ashamed, feeling like my thoughts are stamped all over my face. They leave finally...it takes roughly 3 minutes, but that is a long ass time when you feel like you are slowly dying.

I can finally breathe again.

Once I get my bearings I book it up the stairs and dig through my junk drawer, bobby pins, lip chap, random papers go flying left right and center, until I finally find my stash of pot, and a little 1 hitter pipe. My hands are still trembling; I nervously pack the pipe as full and as tight as I can. Once packed, I gingerly open my window as wide as it will go. I carefully close my door, and shove a towel at the bottom to fill the crack between the door and the floor. I draw the curtains around me so I am cocooned between the curtains and the window. I can't let my parents find out I am smoking weed, let alone smoking in their house. I light the pipe, suck it in and hold it. I choke a couple of times,

Come on you lightweight, hold this shit in.
You need this

I exhale. Followed by a terrible 2 min of coughing and choking. God, dry old weed sucks, but hell, it will do the trick.

Ahhh, I can breathe again. Chin up, tits out I coach myself in the mirror again. As I reapply perfume and fix my lipstick.

I really hate lipstick and shaky hands.

I regroup myself, and look at the time. I have about fifteen minutes or so, I got this!

Five minutes pass. Wow that is it?
I decide to phone my younger brother. I don't know how he will help, but chances are he is stoned too, and can talk some stoner nonsense into me.

First ring he picks up. "Soooooooo...I heard you kicked mum and pop out of the house, well done!

"Ugh, they wouldn't leave fast enough" I sighed out on a long exhale, still choking on that dry terrible weed.

"Well, did you smoke a little ganja yet?"

"Yes, it didn't do jack shit"

"Well smoke some more, I am on my third b-rip A.T.M."

"Third bong rip? Lucky bastard" I managed to sneak in a small chuckle as I started to pack another pipe with my overly annoying shaky hands.

Light the pipe.

My brother thinks he is too cool for school and thinks he is actually a gangster. He is a pasty ass white boy, with blonde hair and blue eyes. He stands at 6 foot 4 and weighing in at 130 pounds soaking wet gangster. With better brand recognition and shopping habits than I do. Yes, he is delusional, but I love him!

Cough; cough... because I have to.

Inhale.

Hold it in.

Exhale... followed by another round of choking on that horrible smoke.

"Feel better yet?" He asks after my couple second silence

"I think so." I managed to spit out in between coughs and chokes.

"So where are you guys going anyways? Taking you out to a 5 star place?"

"Ivory, it is an East Indian buffet"

"Ohhh....yay! Watch out for that explosive diarrhea after eating all that foreign shit."

"Thanks for the vote of confidence there bro"

"You are MIGHTY welcome sista gurlll"

Like I said... gangster.

"When is he coming to get you?"

"Any minute now"

Ugh, I can feel the panic start to set in again. The thumping is once again becoming defining. My chest tightens and speeds up. My hands start to sweat so much, they start to leak. Yes, leak!

"K. Go smoke another pipe, 911 text me if you need out. Don't forget to brush your teeth. Have fun. Oh yeah, don't forget condoms."

How does my younger brother calm me down like that? I am supposed to be the wiser, older, calmer one. Telling him that everything will be okay and giving him sisterly advice. But nope, on the other hand, he is telling his mental basket case broken older sister that she'll be okay.

We hang up, and then I wipe my wet hands on my house coat that is hanging off the back of my door to dry them off in order to pack my last pipe. I smoke the last pipe, clean myself up, tidy up the evidence in my room and stare out my room window watching a strange car pull up into my driveway.

How the fuck did I end up in a place like this? Who am I? What the fuck am I going to do?

This is a pretty fucking crazy story, a lot of really bad shit happened. But with the entertainment of my alter ego, the support of my crazily eccentric family, psychotic friends, a shit ton of pot, and literally barrels of wine, I survived it.

My name is Hadley Hope McLeary, and this is my story.

I met Riaan for the very first time at a fair in Winnipeg that visited every summer. I look back often and wonder if it were too much too soon, or if there was anything I could have done to control the way things turned out. I think a lot about that these days. There is nothing I would change, though. For some reason, I believe in 'Kizmit' (as my mum loves to call it). I only believe in it because she's changed part of my perspective on the way things have happened. She only started believing in kizmit after her accident when my brother Blake and I were much younger. I believe that most of the decisions I would have made regarding my situation would probably have led up to the same result. Riaan was a bright point in my life that I'm not sure I would ever give up if given a choice.

CHAPTER ONE

Panty Soup

July 2007

"Hadley."

"Hmm," I responded, staring at the boxes at our feet.

"This...This is the business?"

My mum looked surprised, staring at the same boxes I was looking at. I was also surprised by what made up the business that I had just bought with my mum; seven large Rubbermaid containers. Not what I expected, but I had worked with Miss Muir for the past two summers before deciding to buy her out. What can I say? She had a good business proposal.

"Mum, it's going to be amazing. I can tell," I said, hugging myself with a bright smile. "And you'll love it."

"I'm not questioning the business, it's Just—" She paused.

"Just what?" I asked, eagerly.

"Nothing Hun. I'm just excited seeing you take your first step into the business world."

"So exciting. And I'll be able to pay my way through college. Imagine that!"

Growing up for me was the best experience I ever had. There were the good days, and then there were the bad days, but knowing that my mum and dad were always there with an encouraging word or two made my childhood amazing. That same support system was one of the things that made going into business with my mother an exciting prospect, with my parents' individual successes serving as great motivators. I wanted to be just like them; successful, rich, and comfortable in my own skin.

I spun around in glee. It was happening. I was an independent adult with a car, and a business, and everything was falling into place.

I adjusted the paint bottles for the tenth time that morning, and surveyed the entire booth while Samara stood off in a corner regarding me with amusement. I ignored her. She found it funny that I bothered with arranging things.

"You know everything will be a mess again with the next wave of customer's right?" She asked, sauntering to me.

I turned with a laugh. "Right? Fuck, I shouldn't have bothered."

"Nah, it's good. This way we look serious," she said with a grin.

It was another day at one of the summer fairs in Winnipeg, and we were making good money so far. I felt great because I had proven myself. Buying this business had been a brilliant idea. The booth was very popular, and we had made back the initial investment for our business already. One of the things I really loved about working there was the people I met daily.

The flirting was a side attraction, and a very compelling one.

As hungry as I was for attention, I was even hungrier for success.

Sitting close to the entrance of our booth, joking around, and keeping an eye out for people who happened to give our booth a second look, I was mildly peeved when Samara's leg flew out of left field, knocking me in the shin.

Yo bitch, what the fuck?!

"Ouch, what the hell?" I exclaimed.

"Do you see those?" She gawked, not even trying to be discreet.

I turned curiously, wondering what had caught Samara's eyes. It was a beautiful sight. A group of guys dressed alike in dickies shorts, red shirts, and sunglasses strutted down the aisle.

"Yup, I definitely see those." I murmured quietly, and attempting to smile too. They sauntered by us, almost in slow motion while giving us nods of acknowledgement.

"Panty soup, panty soup," she drooled.

I could only stare after them in fascination before what Samara said struck me. Panty soup? What was that? And suddenly a light bulb went off in my head.

It's my vagina drooling. She was right!

"Um, yeah, can I go on my break now? I think I need to go to the bathroom and find something to eat."

I turned to her with a raised brow and a knowing smirk. She smiled sheepishly.

"Good God, just go." I said. "Be back in thirty minutes though. After that, it's my turn."

When it was my turn to go and skulk out the fair for those beautiful specimens, I booked it out of the booth. I turned the corner of the tent in black Steve Madden sling backs, and then I walked right into someone.

Seriously? Get the fuck out of my way!

Trying to get my bearings, I looked up and this man appeared with kind, sparkling honey brown eyes that seemed to be looking directly into my soul. It gave me an instant sense of peace and comfort. My vision widened, and looking at his face felt like a drawing being filled in. First his hair, then his lips as he stretched out a helping hand to me.

"I am so sorry. Are you okay?" He asked in a beautiful accent that made my heart flutter. After helping me to my feet, he continued apologizing and asking if I were okay, but I wasn't. I feel as though I'd been knocked off my feet. Figuratively.

I nod drunkenly, not quite sure of what I'm answering. "I'm okay. I'm great. Totally my fault. I wasn't paying attention to where I was going, and I turned the corner too fast. My bad."

"No, no. That was completely my fault. I'm glad this happened though. I saw you earlier on my break and was on my way back to say hi. Just glad I caught you before you disappeared. You've been on my mind."

I've been on your mind? Oh my God, oh my God, oh my God!

"Oh really?" I tried playing it cool. "I was actually just going to grab a bite to eat." I said as I pulled the base of my short shorts down over the bottom of my booty, trying to look sexy. I probably looked a mess, but I definitely did not feel it.

"Great! I'm on my supper break as well. Would you like to join me?" He asked.

That day we walked, ate, and chatted for almost an hour. His name was Riaan Olfert. He was four years older than me and from South Africa. I had originally thought he was Australian, which he explained to me was practically an insult because it suggested a lack of culture. He was working at the fair with his best friend, and traveling through Canada and the United States for nine months before going back home. He was a carny, and it was an amazing new strategy getting all these gorgeous hunks to work at the fair. They definitely caught my attention.

Riaan and I became completely enamored with each other. That one hour changed our lives. His perspective on life was something completely new to me. His life story excited me in ways I didn't realize a story could. It was like this whole new world had been shown to me within an hour of talking to a stranger. That whole night, and everything about it was so surreal from the lights flashing making me feel woozy and almost epileptic; the rides whirling around us making the big engines barrel out a constant hum. The sirens, bells, and whistles at the games turned into a persistent buzz and vibration in my eardrums. The bass of the music at each ride made my heart match its beat; I could feel the bass in my chest, and the butterflies swirling in my stomach to the tune. It was as if I was in a sort of dream; I could not comprehend if this feeling was actually real, or if it was just in my head. This man gave me a feeling that I did not know existed from the moment I laid eyes on him. It was a bit frightening.

We spent the next seven days together, and every moment we could get away from our duties at the fair. Every bathroom break I could take, I would book it to his ride just to sneak in a quick glance at this angel on earth that was actually into me. He'd give me a quick wink and a small one-side smile. He had the cutest dimples whenever he smiled, and it melted my heart every time. He would come to my booth every morning, and we would set up together. We would laugh, flirt, and joke. We would hold hands every chance we got and sneak in kisses when no one was looking. Every meal at the fair was date time; it was our time, regardless of how busy, or quiet my booth was. My hunger for success faded. My hunger for more of Riaan was deep and consuming.

When the fair came to an end, we made it a point of planning one proper date without work hanging over our heads. I drove to the empty lot where a mere sixteen hours prior the biggest carnival in the province was. It was littered with empty food containers, confetti, and partially deflated balloons floating like half-mast flags announcing a death. The carnival was over, and we both didn't't know

where this was going to go. Was this lust af-
fair we endured over the last seven days going
to end this evening? Who knew, but tonight,
it would be one last good night. I had worn
my best matching bra and panties along with
the cutest dress I had that year. I had thrown
a handful of condoms in my purse that morning before leaving the house as well. I knew I
was going to get me a piece of this. I was
hopeful all week, and tomorrow he would
leave. This was my last chance, and I would
not leave until the fireworks went off.

The fair grounds were depressing. There
was an underlying anxiety that the looks of it
gave me. I ignored it.

We went to The Keg for an amazingly de-
licious supper. We sat next to each other as
opposed to sitting across the table, our arms
wrapped up together. My legs draped over
his, and his hand rubbed my inner thigh as we
spoke and flirted. We spent a few hours at the

restaurant eating, drinking, kissing, rubbing, and touching. The night flew by too fast. It was almost midnight when we wrapped up our dinner. I went to the bathroom while he was paying for the bill.

I strutted my stuff knowing he was probably checking out my ass as I walked to the bathroom. My intention was to put an even clearer message for where I intended this night to end. In the bathroom, I rummaged through my purse to find my make up to do a quick touch up. The thought of the night ending soon allowed the anxiety to creep up again.

You got this. Why are you worried? It has been a week. It will not be the end of the world if I don't see him again. Ugh, my gut is turning, why am I worried about him leaving?

I looked at myself in the mirror blinking back tears of anxiety.

"Chin up, tits out!" I muttered. I surveyed myself critically in the mirror, and smoothed out the fabric of my dress. I breathed in with satisfaction at how I looked, spun on my heel, and walked out of the bathroom.

This is it babe. Tonight is your night babe. I said to myself while picturing Danny DeVito in the 90's movie Twins with Arnold Schwarzenegger. Tonight is your night babe.

We hopped into my car, which was essentially an extension of my living space; I had a minimum of three pairs of shoes in the car at all times, extra panties, and a ton of other things. I had cleaned it out however, in preparation for tonight.

The emptiness of the carnival parking lot was consuming and loud. It gave me a jolt of anxiety through my stomach, and the thought of saying goodbye made me nervous. I parked by the gate where I had to drop him off. I put the car in park and tilted my hips to him. His arm crept up close to my face. He rubbed his thumb down my cheek, and then gently pulled my face towards his as he kissed my cheek and whispered into my ear, "How about we find a dark corner away from here?"

I angled my face towards his to gently smooch his cheek and nodded yes. I threw the car into first gear, pulled back from his grasp, and started to crawl towards the nearest darkest spot of the parking lot.

We found a perfect spot; put the car into park, turned on some music in the background. It was an odd mix of music, a little Bob Sinclair and Ice Cube, mixed with Norah Jones and Frank Sinatra, and every now and then Bob Marley, or ACDC would show up. I can't help but like an array of music. Sometimes I feel like wearing the Rasta hat, and sometimes I dwell on my childhood with Classic Rock, and I could not help that I love the

90's RnB. It was a constant surprise on what
worked for me at that moment. I made a habit
of pressing shuffle on my playlist, and then
letting it go to town. As soon as the music situation was nailed down, it was time for me to
get nailed.

Pun intended.

I hopped in the back seat of my car, and
threw the back seats down so we had the entire back of the car as space. There were no
close lights in range— only enough to see
shadows in the crevasses, and curves of our
bodies. He climbed back behind me as he
pulled his shirt over his head. There was no
need to make small talk anymore. We were
about to get down and dirty.

As great as the Caliber was, it was still a
compact small SUV. There was room to pack
stuff in, but to maneuver two full grown bodies in the back mingling, and intertwining

with each other was challenging. After a couple of elbows to the head, and knees in the groins we found a perfect angle to make it all work.

It was so surreal looking back on it; we steamed up the windows, hot sweaty bodies moving with the slow bass of the music in the background. It was like having an outer body experience, watching from above; our bodies swaying with each other moving together sometimes like one. He tasted sweet and fresh. It reminded me of the beach, like a sweet mix of coconut, sand, and a slight sea breeze.

After what seemed like mere minutes, our hot sweaty bodies collapsed onto one another finishing in a bit of a cuddle. He leaned in and smooched my forehead and promised me that this would not be the last time we would see each other. Then, even without any proof that he would keep his promise I didn't second-guess it. It felt as though everything would be all right somehow.

It took everything to say goodbye that night. It took everything I had to keep the tears back. For some reason, one kept sneaking out. Riaan would slightly giggle, wipe it away gently, and give me a soft sweet kiss. Those kisses were the ones that made me feel complete inside. They melted my heart and gave me tingles from head to toe.

He left the next day off to the next big city to run the next big fair. I did not know when or how I would see him again, but driving home, besides the little bit of tears, I knew deep down inside it was not the end of Hadley and Riaan.

CHAPTER TWO

Kizmit

A few weeks had passed since the fair left Winnipeg, and every so often I would catch myself staring off into space with an absent minded smile. The first couple days had been a little difficult as I had still not heard from Riaan, but I brushed it off and refocused on working and preparing for college in the fall. It had been a blissful week, but all good things naturally come to an end.

"Hadley," Gwen called one evening. "I've got a business proposition for you."

I laughed as I shut the front door. "Mum, would you at least let me get in the door first?"

"No, no, no. This, you definitely want to hear."

"Okay," I replied, curiously. "What is it? As long as we're making some money I'm definitely interested."

"So I made some phone calls today and got us into K-days." Mum smirked. We both knew that it was the next big festival for Riaan to attend. It was also three times the size of the festival at home, which meant three times the money.

I was not your typical eighteen-year old, but there were times when I got excited and acted my age. This was one of those times.

"Really?" I jumped up, and knocking my chair over, flew across the room to hug her. "Oh my God, Mum, we're going to have such a great time! I can't wait! When do we leave?"

"We have a shit ton to do, but we will be leaving in about a week. We'll spend the two weeks at your aunt and uncle's house and drive out to the fair and work 16 hour days. You think you can handle that?"

Ha! Yeah, work every day. My man would be there, and that was our time.

"Handle that? Can *you* handle that? We are going to be rich, and I get to see Riaan again. Oh mum, mum, mum, do you know how excited I am about that?" I squealed jumping around, and flitting from place to place.

"Yes dear, you've been a miserable brat the last three weeks, and the idea came to me in a dream last night that we should go into K-days."

My mum believes in kismet. She strongly believes that her dreams predict the future after, a nearly fatal accident she had. Her belief only strengthened when she had a dream of a close friend of hers being diagnosed with cancer, and dying. It eventually happened. Most of the times she mentioned kismet I barely paid attention, but this time I was definitely listening.

She dreamt of joining K-days, and it was meant to be. We were going to be successful and make money, but more important than that— something great would happen with Riaan and me. This time around her dream excited me instead of the typical eye roll, and nod in agreement of her crazy ideas.

So, we packed up our stuff and set out west to the festival. Upon our arrival in the city, excitement started to build up in the bottom of my stomach. As we drove to the festival I could see the merry-go-rounds and the large roller coasters from blocks away. My hands started sweating with anticipation as we got closer to our destination to unload.

How am I going to find him? What's going to happen? Will he be excited to see me? Would he be as happy as I am about this?

Those thoughts kept running through my mind like a staccato beat as I fidgeted in the passenger seat.

We pulled up to our booth, and started to unpack the vehicle. Every load I made my eyes darted around every inch of the grounds I could see. No dice. No Riaan. Something deep in me started to panic thinking that I wouldn't see him.

Once we finished unpacking the vehicle and setting up our booth, I slumped with a huff into the closest chair, disappointed that I didn't get a chance to see him. My mum sighed gustily. "To be young and in love. Would you like to take a walk around the park and look for him?"

My eyes lit up.

"Of course I would love that." I jumped to my feet, hopping forward, and dragging my mum. The hunt was on now.

It was easy to find his ride. It was called the "Fireball," and it was the loudest most popular ride on the midway. It was bright pink, and white, super hard to miss, but naturally I couldn't find that stupid fucking pink ride. We searched up and down every (or what we thought was every) corner of the fair to no avail. There was no sign of him. Because the fair wasn't starting for a couple of days, none of the guys were wearing their uniforms. I couldn't recognize anyone from back home.

"Honey," My mum started, sensing the misery building in me. "Maybe his ride isn't here yet. We are here for 2 weeks. If it is meant to be, you'll find him."

"Mum! Seriously, you dreamt about this, which means it IS meant to happen. He will just have to find me. Or some shit." I started to drag my feet on the pavement. My mum smacked the back of my head in response.

"Don't do that. You'll ruin your nice shoes."

My hands flew up in the air, and spun in a circle losing my balance a bit. I regained my balance when I saw a guy wave at me from a distance. I squinted in an attempt to figure out who this stranger waving at me was. I didn't recognize him, but as he walked towards us I figured I must have been mistaken. Maybe he had been waving at my mum. When he reached us, he stopped and stuck his hand out towards me.

"You must be Riaan's gal," he said, smiling widely. "He hasn't shut up about you in the past few weeks, and he was hoping you would be here. Love birds, ya?"

I blushed brightly. My heart started to pound with relief and joy. He was here, and had told his friends about me.

"Hi, I'm Gwen, Hadley's mum. And who might you be?" My mum demanded.

"Oh shit, how rude of me. My mum would give me a good slap for my bad manners. My apologies. I'm Pieter. Pieter Van De Merve, ma'am." He took her hand, shook it, and then proceeded to lay a soft kiss on the back of it.

My mother blushed, not like a dusky rose, but sixty shades of cherry red. Pieter stood at a whopping six foot six with dark brown hair, and piercing blue eyes that anyone could get lost in. They were like crystal blue pools filled with life, mystery, and my mum was tickled pink by his courteousness.

"Please don't call me ma'am, Pieter. I am not that old. Call me, Gwen." She waved it off, threw her head back and hooted.

Hooted. My mum actually hooted.

I turned to Pieter. "So, is Riaan around? We just finished setting up and were just taking a stroll to see everything. It'll be a big week here."

I tried playing it cool, but my squeaky voice did little to hide my excitement. Neither did bouncing testily on my toes.

"Oh, yeah. He isn't here right now. His truck got a flat so he's a day out. Really Hadley, you've changed my buddy, and I don't know what you did, but he hasn't been the same since he met you. He won't stop talking about you, and he drags me to every tattoo shop, at every show trying to find you. The worst part is always when we can't find you. It's painful." A varying set of expressions ran across his face while his hands fluttered expressively. "I'm missing out on all the parties helping him look for you."

Mum and I walked around the grounds with him for a little bit. He had explained that he was Riaan's best friend, and they had grown up together in South Africa. They both had decided to do this trip together to make some extra cash and experience North America a little bit. It was their third month out of a long nine months, and they both hated the lifestyle already. They worked long hard hour's every day and went without any days off for weeks. They lived in semi-truck trailers that were renovated into bunks, with a horrible diet that consisted mostly of Mr. Noodles and Mid-way Pizza. He also mentioned that they had been struggling to keep on weight because they were working so much and did not have enough time to eat properly during the days. I felt awful for them.

That night after socializing with my aunt and uncle, who were hosting us for two weeks, I laid on my air mattress in the spare room and fantasized about what it would be like tomorrow to see Riaan for the first time in three weeks. The slow motion run towards one another, the wind blowing in our hair as we reached each other, and then wrapped our arms around each other in a tight embrace. Everyone around us then would start a slow applause as a cute love song started playing in the distance. I fell asleep that night with a big smile on my face.

And definitely a happy vagina.

The next morning I was up before my alarm. I showered, and scrubbed every nook and cranny, sprayed on my favorite perfume, and took an extra-long time to play with my makeup. I even tried doing the smoky eye trick, but failed multiple times. After the third try, I gave up. Who had five hours in the morning to do make up? I didn't.

When we got to the fair, all I wanted to do was break free and to find Riaan's ride. The anticipation was killing me. I'd barely slept the night before. My heart pounded so fast, it was hard to swallow over the knot in my throat. I couldn't even answer the simple question my mum asked me.

"Coffee?"

"Sorry... I missed what you just said?" My feet reached the ground again. My head was

so far up in the clouds that reality didn't ex-
ist. I was head over heels for this guy, and I
couldn't even function.

My mum repeated her question again, annoyed. "Would you like a cup of coffee?"

"Oh, yeah. Could I go get them for us?" My
mind quickly raced to the thought of the
slight chance I could run around the entire
fair and look for the ride to see whether I
could find my angel.

"Nope, I will go for a walk and find the coffee for us. I need the fresh air, and the walk
will do my back good before starting to work
all day."

"Fine," I muttered, annoyed.

"You'll see him, promise." She stated firm-
ly, giving me that mum look.

As we turned the corner, I was supposed to go right to the booth, her turning left to go find coffees, but stopped when I recognized the figure standing there.

Riaan.

I looked back at my mum who merely smiled and winked at me.

My smile widened so much that it almost hurt my cheeks. The light caught his eyes as they made contact with mine— those beautiful honey brown eyes. I ran down to my booth, and leaped into his arms. He wrapped his arms around my waist while I wrapped my legs around his waist. I gave him the hardest kiss I had ever given. Fireworks shot off in every inch of my body, tiny little explosions of excited tingling. I had no idea how, or why I was feeling this way, but it felt amazing, and it felt right. I felt like I was where I was supposed to be. I felt like I belonged in his grasp.

Riaan and I jumped apart laughing when my mum cleared her throat loudly behind us. As she nudged me aside and went in for a hug of her own with Riaan, he wrapped his arms around her and planted a big kiss on her cheek.

"Hey there, Mrs. McLeary. Missed ya lots."

The greeting we'd had was everything I had imagined it would be and so were the following two weeks. We spent every waking moment possible together. He would set up with my mum and I in the morning and bring us lunch and supper during his breaks. At the end of our day, we would swing by his ride with a snack. Sometimes if it wasn't a busy day, he would make arrangements with his co-workers and spend the night with us.

The first night he stayed over, we spent some time with my aunt, a bottle of Grand Marnier, and cups of tea. After everyone had gone to bed, we snuggled up on the couch and talked about life, and made jokes about random things. After some time, I got drowsy and wriggled even closer to him. The warmth and the comfort of him being there lulled me into an even more relaxed state. Just as I was about to drift away, I felt his lips brush across my forehead.

"I love you."

A warm blanket of hope, pleasure, and comfort enveloped my body.

"I love you too." I whispered.

Two nights after Riaan told me he loved me, my mum and I had just worked a particularly busy day at the fair. We made it home pretty exhausted, but after everyone went to bed, I took several handfuls of cash, plugged the bathtub drain, and sat down in it. I leaned back so my back was against the wall, and my legs were stretched out. Then, I threw the lumps of bills in the air and let them scatter and rain down on me. At the side of the tub, I had *Make It Rain* playing very low. I was drunk on both love and money.

Riaan and I never talked about what would happen once this fair was done. The summer was nearing an end, and his route wasn't passing through my city anymore. We both knew it was a conversation we would need to have eventually, and we did, reluctantly. We saved it for the last day of the fair. Tears streamed down my face the entire morning.

I was completely head over heels in love with this guy, and lost my entire cool. I would look at myself in the mirror and cry knowing that I would be leaving soon and wouldn't know when I would see him again, or *if* I would ever see him again. I was devastated.

"So, I have been thinking," Riaan said, quietly. "I didn't want to ever leave South Africa,

but with the last two weeks we have spent together. I can't imagine my life without you
now. Canada does sound like a cool place to
live. I would do anything for you, to be with
you. So let's do that. You down?"

Yes, it was as simple as that. I was totally
down!

"Yeah, I think that is a great idea. Canada
is great, I love it here, and my family is all
here. We could do really great things here.
We could build an empire together." I squeaked with excitement.

"Then, the plan is settled. I want you to
meet my family. Let's make a plan for when I
get home after my trip is completed so you
can meet my folks, and then I can start to
immigrate to Canada. Does Christmas on the
beach sound all right to you?" He chirped.

Me? Go to South Africa? Oh. My. God! Me little miss small town is up, up, and away to Africa? Unreal!

It didn't feel like reality. The butterflies and the excitement were like nothing I had ever felt before.

"See ya on the flip side."

CHAPTER THREE

Roughing it

African Style

Have you ever been so excited and so nervous at the same time that you wanted to cry, puke, and jump up and down all at the same time? That was me the entire week prior to me leaving to visit my angel in South Africa. I was planning on spending two weeks there over my Christmas break from College.

College started great. The group of people that I was going to school with was made up of intelligent individuals that really pushed me to my academic limits. Some days, I came home my mind blown on the theories, and ideas that were discussed in class. Every chance I had I mentioned Riaan and I, along with our romantic love story. I made up reasons out of nowhere just to talk about Riaan, and how much I was infatuated with him. People politely nodded, but rolled their eyes once I turned my head. I chattered nonstop about his gorgeous eyes, or his charming accent. Love is truly blind, we have all been there, and if you haven't, believe me, you are really truly doing your family and friends a favor.

When the day finally came, I had two rolling suit cases, an oversized purple Louis Vuitton bag, and a passport purse. I was excessively over-packed. I had half a suitcase full of shoes. I was completely oblivious on how stupid I looked. Once my parents and I got to the airport, my nerves went flying. After multiple conversations revolving around if I were ready, and prepared, and going to be safe, and all that jazz that concerned parents said to their daughter, my parents started to blubber on me.

Ugh, why do they have to be so emotional? If my parents cry, I cry. I just can't help it. Watching my dad cry,.... I mean come on... what daughter in their right mind can look at their dad and not start to bawl themselves? Heartless bitches, that's who. And as tough as I thought I was, I wasn't a heartless bitch, so I started to cry so hard. I even had snot bubbles come out of my nose.

"Be smart," my dad said, a tear streaming down his cheek.

"Be safe, and have fun!" My mum caressed my face, her own nose red from crying.

"Thanks, Fasha," I blubbered out and reached in for a hug.

For some reason, my family loved the Austin Power's string of movies. Even to the point of having multiple Austin Powers parties with fifty plus people from the neighborhood dressed up as Austin Power's characters. We had the local grocery store owner come over dressed up as Fat Bastard one year. My parent's costumes fluctuated year by year, but the best was when my dad ran around as Gold Member flaunting his "gold member" through the zipper of his pant— which had a large cucumber from the garden painted gold, and naturally my mum dressed up as a Fem-bot with funnels painted silver on her chest. I always said "Fasha" like Gold Member did while trying to pronounce "father."

I gave my mum a kiss and waved them off as I walked through security. I was so excited that my stomach hurt. I had never traveled outside of North America before, let alone travel by myself. This was a huge journey for me.

I had three flights to get me to South Africa, and then a small puddle jumper to get me to the beach coast city I was staying at. My flight from Europe landed late, so I had only forty-five minutes to get off the international flight, go through customs, grab my bags, and then race to find the domestic wing of the airport re-check in, check my bags in again, go through security, again, and then run to my gate to board the plane.

As I was going through security, I heard them do a last boarding call for my flight. My heart sank to the pit of my stomach, and I started to sweat. I was in a fucking pink sun dress, heels, and had more bags than anyone should be allowed to have, and all this god-

damn travel just for me to miss my last GD
flight.

Hell no!

I finally reached my gate where they took
one look at my ticket. "Ah, we have been
waiting for you Miss McLeary. You're late!" A
tall skinny black woman sneered at me.

*Like it was my fucking fault? My God
damn plane from Europe arrived late because
the plane had to get diced, or some shit. I ran
my ass off in your God forsaken hot ass airport.*

I was sweating in places I didn't even know
I had at this point. Sweat dripped down my
forehead, the back of my legs, and I had some
serious boob sweat issues. I didn't even have
big boobs to begin with. I looked atrocious.

As I stepped onto the plane, almost everyone was seated and settled. I searched the aisle for my seat when I started to notice all the impatient eye rolls coming my way. Then, I started to notice that all those impatient eye rolls were coming from nothing but black people. I realized then also that everyone on the plane *was* in fact, black, which in turn made me the only white person on the plane.

Now, I was raised not to see color and judge it. I never was in a situation where it was ever pointed out to me in a negative way. But, I also lived in Canada, where I was the majority, and I had never been in a classroom, or a transit bus, or even a house party where I was the only white person. This was a new one for me, and all of them were gawking, and sneering at me as though I was the reason the flight was late. Well, I was the reason the flight was late, but it wasn't my fault.

I finally found my seat, but found someone already sitting in it. The man was in his forties and sitting in my seat with what seemed to be his two friends. I double checked my ticket, and looked at the seat number again. Then as politely as I could, I asked, "Excuse me, sir. Does your ticket say 17F as well?"

I smiled trying to be charming. At this point the three guys were staring at me, hard. I could feel their irritation radiate. I started to sweat even more.

"Yeah, this is my seat. What did you do now?" He snapped.

"Oh sorry, you know there must be a misprint, no biggie. I will ask the crew for help." I stuttered out.

"I ain't moving my ass for you white girl. You already made us late!" He kissed his teeth and rolled his eyes. He leaned back then, and crossed his arms at his chest.

I gingerly smiled and took a few steps back scared out of my mind. As I turned around to look for a crew member, I found myself face to face with one.

"Is there a problem here? You ARE holding us up, and we would like to get in the air since you have made us late already." She snapped, hands on her hips and lips pursed.

Oh shit.

"Sorry ma'am there must be a misprint on my ticket, as this gentleman has the same seat number on his." I said, as charmingly as possible.

She checked both our tickets before looking to the man with a charming smile. "Well, sir, I am sorry for this inconvenience. Let me move you up to first-class. My apologies for this disturbance."

Racist bitch. Oh, shit! Did that thought just come to my head. My mother would kill me if she heard that.

So, she moved him to first-class, and left his two buddies behind.

Smooth move, ex-lax.

"Sorry excuse me guys, could I get into the seat now? Please and thank-you!" I perked up in hopes that the guys would move out of their seats so I could grab the now empty window seat.

"Like hell you can, you have been nothing but an annoyance. You can crawl over if you want this seat." This guy looked at me with a smirk of excitement that suggested he enjoyed being rude.

What the hell have I gotten myself into? And why did everyone hate me?

The last flight was 45 minutes long, and by far it was one of the longest 45 minutes of my life ever. I silently cried the entire way. When we finally landed, the fear and anxiety had subsided, and the excitement started to crawl back up. We hit the ground, and between the bounces of the tires on the tarmac I almost squealed with excitement. Once off the plane, I kept my head down, and my eyes to myself as best as I could while racing to the baggage claim.

I could not wait to see Riaan. It had been months since I had seen him last, and I couldn't believe this was finally the moment. To be exact it had been a hundred and twelve days.

He was looking better than ever when I finally spotted him through the crowd. His eyes sparkled in the light, and his smile was so wide his ears got in the way.

I bee-lined it through the crowd of people until I reached him. Once I reached him, I almost collapsed into his arms in relief. It was almost uncanny, but I couldn't believe as soon as I felt his touch, my body just released all its stress. I sank into him. His embrace was so warm and powerful that it recharged me and made me feel whole again. He showered me in kisses and hugs and an endless string of "I love yous."

We drove along the south coast for a couple of hours. The scenery was breathtaking to say the least. The ocean crashed on the right side in rolling waves, and with surfers off in the distance carving through the monstrous waves. On the left side, there were mountains with gravel paths winding through them. Every time we slowed down to go through a residential area, our truck would be bombarded with a handful of little kids with trinkets and fruit to sell us.

"Miss! Miss! Want to buy? Good fruit?"

"Miss! Miss! African carvings..." They all chirped at my windows.

"How cute!" I squeaked, looking at them. I just wanted to steal them all and take them home. They were adorable.

"Ew, no! They smell, and they steal from you if you aren't careful. Keep your windows up, Hadley, my dear. Just look forward. It is safer that way. I want to keep you safe here," Riaan started to snap out, but then quickly turned down his tone. He finished his comment looking into my eyes with genuine concern and protectiveness.

"Oh, okay. I didn't know. They remind me of those kids in those commercials on TV," I said in a quiet, almost disappointed voice. He was why I was here, and this was his home. He would tell me what was right and wrong here. I didn't want to get us into any trouble. He had warned me before that there weren't any safe places here. In the end, it *is* still Africa.

We finally reached the small-gated community that he and his parents lived in. We pulled up to the gate, and he pulled out a small remote control, taped together, and worn out.

"This is the remote that will let us into the complex, without it we are locked out. It keeps all the black out, and all the dangerous people." He said.

What the hell?

I had thought all the "gated communities" in Africa were to keep out the dangerous animals, like lions, or crocodiles, and such. Not the people. But what did I know? I was just a little ol' white girl in Africa with no clue what I had gotten myself into. So, I played it as cool as possible.

We pulled up into the driveway of a tall skinny white and sage green cement house with bars on all the windows and doors. It looked like a small jail building, but it was home for the next couple of weeks. As soon as I opened the door, and stepped out, I caught sight of this sad, decrepit, blob of a woman hobble towards me with her arms wide open.

Riaan's mother was a bit different. He had warned me about her. She was a cancer survivor, but she smoked a pack of cigarettes a day, and did some serious damage on a box of wine every day. She didn't work because she didn't want to work for "those blacks." She was epileptic, bipolar, and just plain nuts. Two weeks prior to my arrival, she attempted to "end it" with a handful of her unlabeled pills, and a box of wine. She overdosed, slipped, and sprained her ankle.

And all this hoopla was because she thought she was too ugly to meet such a pretty girl like me.

"Hadley!" She screamed, practically leaping into my arms. God, she was heavy! "It is so nice to see you! Dad and I have been so excited to meet you. Riaan has said nothing but amazing things about you." She pulled herself back and looked me up and down. "Look at you! Holy fuck, Riaan, Riaan!"

Riaan dropped my bags inside as his mother continued on excitedly, "She is even prettier than you said she was! She is a model. I am going to have beautiful grand-babies!"

Whoa woman, slow down your roll here. Grand babies? Who is talking grand babies? It was going to be a long ass two weeks.

After his mother finished with her minor meltdown while meeting me, a tall lanky man emerged from the house surrounded by two big dogs, a cat on his shoulder, and a cat in his arms.

Who da' hell is this now? Noah's arc or what? Like who just emerges like that, surrounded by animals?

"Hadley, my dear. What a wonderful day today is. I am so very, very pleased to finally meet you! We are oh so happy that you have chosen to come all the way to South Africa to spend Christmas with us. We are so blessed to have you." He said, patting his cat. He sounded exactly like Yoda.

Once settled in and unpacked, I laid down in our room. Riaan climbed in next to me. "I am so sorry about my parents. I told you they were a bit different."

"Ha, ah, ya well...you never said how different." I said, turning to him with a smirk

"So, I have come up with a great idea. I want to take you camping for a part of the week. That way we can get our privacy, and enjoy camping in the African bush. Sound okay?" He smiled. His eyes twinkled happily with his idea.

I was head over heels for this guy. Plain and simple.

"Heck, yes!"

I popped up and smooched him as hard as I could. One thing led to another, and then we were naked.

This is great, having sex for the first time in months, but also with the man you love after not seeing him for months is mind blowing.

We took off the next day to the campground. It was magical, and I couldn't believe it was happening. It was so hot for mid-December. Christmas was right around the corner, and I was used to it being a crisp minus fifty degrees at this point of the year. We set up our camping spot, tent, mattress, and campfire. We had our brandy, and our cooler full of food. We were all set for a week of roughing it Africa style.

Roughing it African style, meant really hot temperature, and a shit ton of thieving monkeys. Those fucking monkeys! Who ever thought monkeys were cute were seriously delusional.

I woke up one morning to some noise outside our tent, and Riaan's arms wrapped tightly around me. I didn't really want to move much, but at the same time I didn't want someone stealing all of our stuff. So I grabbed my camera and turned it on. If someone was going to kill me, or kidnap me I wanted to leave photographic evidence of who it was.

I slowly unzipped the tent, and stuck my camera outside in the direction of where I thought I heard the noise from. I started to snap photos. I retracted my arm to review the photos I took.

Monkeys elbow deep in our cooler of food.

I panicked then kicked Riaan awake. "Wake up! Monkeys are stealing the buns and potato salad!"

I unzipped the tent, and tried to get out, but tripped face first into the ashes of last night's campfire. I lifted my head up to face a monkey, not even an arm's length away from me, with a forty ounce of brandy (my brandy) in its hands — cap off and ready to drink!

This was the exact moment in time when I decided that monkeys were thieving little shits. They looked into your eyes and seared a hole into your soul. I hated monkeys. They were like tiny little vindictive humans covered in fur with blue testicles. Yes, blue testicules.

My last Saturday night in town, Riaan promised me a "top notch" night. His friend dropped us off at this beautiful restaurant that was built in the middle of a swamp. Crocodiles chilled in the distance, and the constant hum and buzz of the African bush was calming and romantic. We enjoyed a beautiful seafood dinner, and I ate way too much. His friend picked us up from the restaurant afterwards, and then took us to the town nightclub.

"Want to get drunk and go dancing?" Riaan asked. He smirked and kissed me deeply, sneaking his tongue into my mouth.

I nodded with the biggest smile on my face. We got to the bar, and immediately threw back two shots of some purple stuff that I had no idea what it was.

Riaan grabbed my hand, and then whispered into my ear, "Wanna try having a little extra type of fun tonight too?"

"What kind of fun are you talking about? I asked excited, yet nervous.

"Well, my buddy gave me a couple of pills of Ecstasy. I would love to take these with you. I promise you it'll be safe, and it will be the best night of your life."

I panicked. "I don't do drugs though. I will become addicted and become homeless and spend all my money on drugs." My hands started to fidget, and run through my hair like a brush. Riaan grabbed my hands and pulled them down. He looked me directly in the eye.

"I promise everything will be perfect. It is our last night together, and we will have an amazing time." He stared so deeply into my eyes, and I instantly felt comfortable. I trusted everything would be okay.

I was right; we popped the pills, chased it with some shot of purple drink again, and let the night transpire. I danced and danced and danced. I was all over the place. I would go up to strangers and introduce myself and have a dance with them and then move on to make new friends. We finished the night on the beach to watch the sunset come up. I had never once stayed up late enough to watch the sunrise come up. I was right at the bottom tip of Africa, and staring out into the ocean. I watched the sun peek over the horizon, dark purple and red, and then meshed with the ocean until no one could tell them apart. It turned into a nice burnt orange and dusty pink shortly after. I could feel the warmth on my face as I closed my eyes to breathe in the moment.

It was honestly one of the best nights of my life.

People say drugs are bad, and yes I agree with them. They are not a healthy or safe life choice. But, what I could say about drugs is that I lost enough inhibition to allow myself to say, experience and feel things that I would have never done otherwise.

The dreadful day came when I needed to go home. It was New Year's Eve, and it would be the longest and most painful flight back home. I didn't know when I was going to see Riaan again. We planned to get Immigration started as soon as I got home. Our plan was to get him on a visiting Visa, and then he would look for a job, and then move the process to permanently living in Canada.

Saying our goodbyes, I sobbed like a child.

I had one of those crying fits, where I had snot bubbles, red swollen eyes, and struggled to breathe between loud sobs. That good bye put the "ugly cry" to shame.

CHAPTER FOUR

To Be or

Not To Be

It had been months since Riaan and I had spent our two weeks in South Africa together. Upon my arrival back home, we immediately started to work on the Immigration process. Both of us underestimated the amount of work, paper collection, and time it took. Not to mention cost of Immigration!

Riaan had applied for his criminal record check, and he also had to reissue his passport because it was almost expired. When he applied for both of the documents, they promised him six weeks before he would get them. Well, six weeks had come and gone, and we were closer to ten weeks, and still no sign of clearance. When he made inquiries about his passport, it turned out that the passport office had lost his original one, and did not have a record of him applying for a new one.

Three months of wasted time and energy.

When we finally got his police clearance back for his criminal record check, it turned out that when one comes through midway, they don't have to send a police clearance through. Otherwise, Riaan would not have been accepted on his work visa. He had not one charge, but two on his record that he had neglected to tell me about because he thought it was no big deal. One was for possession of marijuana on his 18th birthday, and then the second charge was a DUI. So, when we got the response back our thoughts were consumed with fear that he would not be accepted into Canada. The hope that he had been to Canada already, and that these offenses were from a few years back, burned in us. Once we gathered all of his paperwork, and he applied, we were promised another 6-week deadline until we would hear back from Immigration.

At this point, we had been apart for a half a year. Riaan and I were struggling to stay happy, and positive about ever being together. It turned from lovey-dovey romantic happy conversations into small spats here and there. Then, it turned into full blown screaming matches over the phone.

The fair that I met him on the year prior was about to make its stop through my hometown again, and I was prepping on getting my tattoo business all set up to make money. Riaan and I were going days without speaking each other. I was devastated, and so was he. The circumstances were not easy to deal with. The first day of the fair, I was set up, and ready to kick some ass and rake in some cash when I got a text from him.

"Please call me a.s.a.p."

I got my staffer all set up in the booth, and told her I had to run to the car to make an important phone call. I ran anxiously to my car. I wanted to make sure I had good service to make the call across the world, and I also wanted to be somewhere where I could take in what I hoped was excitement.

"Hello? How are you? I got your text and called as soon as I could." I said, breathless.

"I got denied." Riaan said, voice small on the other end of the line.

"What do you mean?" I cracked out. Instantly cries choked my words.

"They denied me, Hadley. I can't come to Canada." He whispered out.

"No, no, no, no, no! We will find another way. There is always a way. I love you, and always will. So, we will find a way." Tears streamed down my face as I tried to hold it in for him. I could tell he was devastated. It broke my heart to feel that pain through the phone, knowing he was in pain, and I couldn't do anything to help him. "We're meant to be together. We will find a way. I promise that everything will be all right."

"No, it won't. I have a record, I was stupid as a kid, and it's now coming back to haunt me. You deserve better, Hadley. You really do. This can't go on. I don't think we'll ever be together." He stuttered out.

"What?" My throat felt like it was kicked in by a steel-toed work boot. Was he doing what I thought he was doing? "You don't have the power to decide what is best for me, or not. I chose you, and I want to be with you. We can and will find another way around this to be together. A work permit? Permanent residence? There are lots of options."

I was so panicked that I was crying and yelling at this point. This only upset him even more.

"Goodbye, Hadley." And he hung up.

I tried calling back multiple times, and it never went through. He had walked out of my life just like that. As I walked back to my booth, I got a text from him saying that he just needed some time to think things through. I couldn't understand what he was asking for. I was so certain of our fate that I didn't see anything else. But now, he just walked away. *Fuck him.*

I stopped at the bathroom on my way back to the booth to fix myself up. I freshened up my face, pulled my boobs as far up as they could go in the top that I was wearing.

Chin up, tits out, Hadley, you got this.

I had plans of strutting my stuff and working my way through this fair whooping ass all around, and who knew, finding some ass of my own. I was going on six months here, and just had my boyfriend walk out on me over a phone call.

As I stepped out of the bathroom, I saw this tall guy with dark curly hair and deep honey colored eyes emerge from the crowd. He had tanned caramel skin, and dense defined muscles that were wrapped with tribal tattoos. As he came closer towards me, I could smell the deep musty man smell— pine and aftershave. The smell made the hairs on the back of my neck stand up. He gave me a wink while I gawked horribly, and then he disappeared behind the men's bathroom door.

A few hours passed with a couple hundred people coming through my booth. I was physically tired, and emotionally exhausted. I was done for the night. When I was nearly done packing up and about to head to my car, someone cleared their throat behind me.

"Excuse me?"

I spun around on my heel to see the guy from earlier that evening.

"Um, hi. How are you?" I stammered out.

"Oh I am just peachy, thanks for asking. I just had to come introduce myself. I saw you earlier today, and you caught my eye." He smiled, a dimple popping up on the corner of his left eye. "My name is Dezzy, and you must be?"

"Oh, I'm, um, Hadley." I said, confused as hell. How did he find me. Was he stalking me?

"Hadley," he said. A shiver went up my spine at the way my name sounded on his tongue, "Have some time to spare for a drink?"

First, I thought hell no. I don't know you, and I have a boyfr— wait, do I have a boyfriend?

Oh, but he was so pretty though. There was a sparkle and a peak of curiosity that was bubbling within me. I was intrigued.

"Well, I guess I could spare some time for a quick drink. Where are you going?"

"Just up the road to the local pub. We're about to head down there now actually," he said.

"Did you want to hop in with me, and I'll take you there?" I asked him.

Dezzy gave a nod. We headed down to the pub together, and met up with about half a dozen of his friends. We had a couple of laughs and even a few shots. Dezzy was up in my business all evening.

He was giving me serious come hither eyes. Oh dear lord, how could I resist those eyes when they are attached to such a defined body, and warm eyes, and not to mention my inner rebel siren was going off... these tattoos... DAMN!

At the end of the night I drove him back to his vehicle, one thing led to another, and it was wam-bam-thank-you-ma'am. My six month dry spell was over. My relationship with Riaan was officially over too.

Riaan called me a few days to apologize for his behavior, and said he wanted us to try a work permit. My heart sank, knowing what I had done a few nights before. I was mortified.

"I am really sorry, baby. I was so caught up with all the negative reaction we were getting from Immigration that I lost hope this time around. But, then a couple of days without you in my life made me realize that I don't want to live without you. Please forgive me. Let's put this all behind us and start fresh with a work permit."

Let's put this all behind us?! I smell a perfect excuse not to tell him everything that happened a couple of nights ago.

"I am happy you came to your senses Riaan," I scolded him so he would not notice how nervous I was. "It's going to be harder to get the work permit ready; we will have to get to work with trying to find you an employer that will sponsor you."

"Okay, you tell me what to do, and I will do whatever I have to do to get to you." He stammered.

CHAPTER FIVE

Machetes,

Machine guns

and a Proposal

The remainder of that year we focused on trying to find Riaan an employer in my city that would sponsor him. I would flip through the yellow pages every day, and call all my connections. Anyone that I knew that hired laborers I thought would be a perfect match. Later in the fall, we had decided since nothing was moving fast with Immigration that it would be a good idea that I go out to South Africa again on my Christmas break from college.

Between work and school, and interviewing with new employers for Riaan, I was extremely busy with life. Before I knew it, I was back on a plane to South Africa. This time around I had emailed the Immigration office in South Africa to see if I could sit down with an Immigration officer to speak to regarding Riaan's file. Over the span of a couple of months, I had sent over five emails and on my way down to South Africa I made sure that I had hard copies of all the e-mails. I was going to go and bust down some doors.

I landed late on a week day evening, and the reunion with Riaan was exactly the same as it was the year before. I was extremely excited to see him and vise versa. We had been apart for eleven and a half months. We were due for some one on one time, especially with how we had fallen apart midsummer.

We stayed at his grandmother's house for a couple of days because it was closer to the Immigration office. His grandmother, Ouma, was a sweet little old lady. She walked with grace and poise and was someone who instantly warmed your heart. When she met me, she bluntly told us that she had been worried that I would be some bimbo, and that it would be hard for her to contain her disappointment in Riaan's choice. She was pleasantly surprised, however, to find that I was smart, and more beautiful than expected. She did make a comment that I was a little "thicker" in person than the photos.

"It's good for making babies." She winked, elbowing my side.

I was under stress and eating for that entire year, and going without sex. Of course, I packed on a couple!

Thank goodness she liked me. She and Riaan were close so I wanted to make sure that she and I got along well.

After getting settled at her house for a couple of days, we found our way to the Immigration office downtown. It was in a really sketchy area, and Riaan was determined to keep me safe. Yet, I was determined to walk into that office and demand answers. We walked up to a rickety old building surrounded by gates and bars with guards standing on either end of the entrance. I pranced up to the front gates, whipped out all the email's I had.

"Excuse me, sir. I have an appointment with an Immigration officer today. Can you please help me?" I asked nicely, big smile on my face.

This giant black man whose neck was the width of my torso looked down at me, gave me the stink eye, and replied, "There is no one here that can help you."

"But I have an appointment. I have been emailing this office for almost two months in regards to my presence today. Surely, there is someone I can speak to in regard to this." I pointed to my e-mails.

He looked straight ahead, and not even at me again.

"There is no one to help you." He said, again.

I started to get flustered at the reception I was getting. People around us started to stare. "Sir, I have come from the other side of the world, and this is my Canadian Embassy! I have every right to be here. Please, can I speak to anyone regarding the Immigration issue we are facing right now?" My voice started to crack. I could feel the tears well up in the back of my throat.

Do not cry. Do not cry! Crying shows weakness. And I am stronger than this man. Like hell I am not going anywhere without speaking with anyone here.

As I stood there, almost on the verge of tears and trying to reason with him, he pulled out his machete with one hand, and then rubbed his machine gun with the other. He stepped forward and looked down upon me. "*There* is *no one* here to see you!"

Riaan grabbed me by the back of my sweater out of the path of the angry guard. "It is time to go, Hadley. It is time to leave. They won't help us here. We will just find another way. Thank you, sir. Have a good day."

"This is not right, Riaan! These people are paid by *my* tax dollars. This isn't right! Who can we go to, to get help now?" I cried out in the car ride home.

"That's how it is here, babe. Black people are out to get the White people. It doesn't matter. We just have to send in the application. They don't talk to people here." He sighed out, rubbing my leg.

"Bullshit!" I said. I crossed my arms as tears streamed down my face.

We spent the remaining of my three weeks in South Africa living in a cloud. We figured we would deal with Immigration when I returned to Canada and enjoy our time together. We had spent so much time apart that it felt so good to finally be back in his arms.

We went on hikes through the African bush, and I got all one with nature. I tried to bounce off a rubber tree, just like George of the Jungle did in that movie with Brendan Fraser. I took a running start at it, and then I walked away after with bruises instead of bouncing off of it. I found dung beetles and weird worms. They were all fascinating. I took hundreds of random photos on our hikes. It was so interesting to me all the weird and foreign things that I found. I found it excessively entertaining to point out funny looking animal genitalia, and sneak a zoomed in photo of animals having sex in the wild.

My favorite to watch was the Rhino's. So many horns.

We completely ignored the fact that I was leaving soon, and that we no longer had a plan for Immigration again once I left. It felt nice to just live in the moment and enjoy having each other face to face. Every evening when we went to bed, we held each other tightly and exchanged hundreds of kisses and 'I love yous' until we fell asleep. When you spend so much time apart, you forget what it feels like to be held, and to be told that someone loves you. It was such a warming feeling. I felt so lucky despite our situation.

Every chance we got we celebrated. We were living in the honey moon phase. We went out for fancy dinners, and went partying for a couple days on end. We did anything and everything that came to mind. One night, we went out with a group of his friends for someone's birthday. They shut down the bar for the private party, and hired a bartender and a DJ just for the group of us. We danced in the flashing lights, took shots upon shots, and in the background of the thumping music our bartender was flipping and juggling bottles. It was a surreal night. Nothing like this would have ever happened at home for me.

This was an experience I would have never had if Riaan were not in my life.

The dreaded day that I was leaving crept upon us way too fast. I blubbered like an idiot again. Snot bubbles and swollen red eyes again. We promised to be patient and kind to one each other and that we would always find a way to be together no matter what. Another thing we did discuss on the way to the airport was if the work permit didn't come through, that we would look into getting married and going through spouse and sponsorship. We figured we should try anything at that point even though our thoughts were that we didn't want to get married just for Immigration purposes. We wanted to get married for the right reasons. We felt that our love was enough to grant that we were getting married to be lifelong partners.

I flew home that year determined to get Riaan back to my home, and start our life together. We were going to figure this out.

Round two started again— the work permit. I finally found a company that produced windows. The owner of the company told me that he would be more than willing to sponsor Riaan here as long as I did all the paperwork and paid for all the fees. He would sign everything that I needed signed. I lucked out with him. Once we compiled all the necessary paperwork, we sent in the application.

This time around, it was a four month waiting period. With all the prior upset with the Immigration office in South Africa, we expected a six to eight-month answer. Surprisingly though, we got an answer within two months. It wasn't the answer we were hoping for again.

"I got denied again, Hadley. They said that they will never accept me on a temporary visa because of our relationship. What do we do?" He asked, defeated.

"Well, it looks like you have a proposal to construct." I said, and then giggled. I was trying to stay positive. I knew it wouldn't be an easy ride to get him here on a permanent visa. We still had his criminal record to deal with, and we both knew that would be an almost impossible task.

"Hadley, my dearest pie. Would you please do me the honor of becoming my wife? So I could hold you, cherish, and love you for the rest of my life?" He asked, whimsically.

I could hear the smile through the phone. I blushed. I knew it was right, and I got so consumed with immediate happiness that I squealed, "Yes, yes, yes, yes, yes!"

"Wonderful, when can you come back to South Africa? How long can you stay? Let's make this a big trip! We have a lot of celebrating to do babe!"

I was graduating from college that summer, and then had the summer to work my business and try to find a full time career move. Or, well at least that was the plan before getting married turned to priority number one. My head went completely to getting married, and everything about it. The rest of my life was put on hold.

Our plan was for me to work the summer, and then go to South Africa for three months. That would give us enough time to get married, and get our marriage certificate. It would also give us a long honeymoon time and give us the time together we deserved. We were eagerly looking forward to being together for longer than a couple of weeks this time around.

Our wedding plans weren't too crazy. We had decided we would have one ceremony to get a marriage certificate ordered quickly, and then we would have a wedding with his family shortly after the first one. Then upon his arrival in Canada, we would have a wedding with all my family. So, not only was I getting married, but I would be getting three celebrations in the name of our wedding. I got to marry my prince charming three times in a row.

The summer blew by, and before I knew it, fall time came. The leaves started to change color, and sometimes there'd be frost on the roofs of the houses in the neighborhood early in the morning. I found a wedding dress from a cute little shop that my mum and I discovered. Riaan's family was paying for the two weddings in Africa. Ouma had offered her house for the first quick ceremony, and the signing of the marriage documents. An aunt and uncle of Riaan's had also offered their backyard to host the second wedding where we would have Riaan's family and friends. It was so exciting that all of it was finally coming together. I was so excited to get married to the love of my life, but one thing kept crossing my mind.

I was doing this all without my parents.

They had been extremely supportive throughout this entire journey with Riaan. When we fought, they'd hug me. When I cried, my mum helped me for hours on end getting all the Immigration documents in line. My dad would go out of his way to spend time with me and purposely ask how everything was with Riaan and I. I knew it hurt them when I was sad about not being with Riaan. I knew watching me do what I was doing at twenty was tough on them. Parents always want the best for their children, and sometimes they never see that anything or anyone is suitable for their children. My parents were supportive. They might not have been one hundred percent about my decisions, but they always told me that they believed that they raised me the "right" way. They trusted my decisions even though they didn't understand, or agree with them. I lucked out that they were awesome with everything.

I grew sad thinking that they weren't going to be there when I said "I do" to this man that they hadn't really spent much time with, just a couple of hours a day for a couple weeks back over two years prior to the wedding with Riaan. A lot had changed, and a lot had grown over that time.

It was about a week before I was to leave for South Africa for three months. I had gotten home from running some errands, and when I walked into the house both of my parents were in the kitchen and called my name.

"Hadley, come here for a sec please." My mum chimed as soon as she heard the door close.

I walked in, not thinking anything important. Maybe just some random fact for the day.

"What's up?" I asked, nonchalantly shrugging my shoulders.

My dad stood up, and looked me in the eye. He studied me intently. I took a step back a bit alarmed. "Hi Fash, what is going on?"

"We should talk. You should sit down for this." He said, gravely. He glanced to the chair for me to take a seat.

Shit, what did I do now?

My dad threw me a bunch of papers. "You should read that, and tell me what it is."

What the hell is going on?

I was in some serious trouble, and had no idea what was going on. I grabbed the papers, and nodded in his direction. I tucked them all nicely so I could read them. I started reading the text with a frown. It was a bunch of numbers and characters not making much sense. Gazing through the page, I saw a reservation code, followed by an airline's name, then flight numbers, and seat numbers.

Oh. My. God.

My heart stopped beating for a moment. "What is this?" I asked, looking my mum in the eyes. My dad scared me. I didn't know how to react to him at that moment.

My dad answered first. "They are flights for your mum, brother, and I to come to your wedding." Then, he finally smirked. A tear fell down his cheek as well.

"Oh, stop it, Sam!" My mum slapped the side of his hip. Tears welled up in her eyes. "Once you start, we all have to fucking start."

"So..." I paused, bewildered at what I just heard. "That means that I will have the three of you at my wedding then?"

"We're going to fucking Africa to play with the monkeys! Ya, Baby, ya!" My mum cheered fists pumping in the air.

My mum is such a dweeb, I love her.

The three of us stood up and gave each other tight hugs and cried and laughed. I was going to have a perfect wedding now. I couldn't wait.

CHAPTER SIX

Priests and Roses

I flew to South Africa with three months' worth of clothing and belongings. I was packed for the trip of a lifetime. My carry on suitcase was my wedding dress carefully rolled up, and I swung it through all the airports with pride and glee. The thirty plus hour trip down to South Africa flew by. Nothing was going to rain on my parade.

I was a pro at traveling this time. I blended in, and had zero problems along the way. Hellsto-the-ya to the comfy Yoga pants I wore. They were a travel must.

I landed later in the evening and was greeted at the airport by Riaan and Ouma. They stood at the gates with a big bouquet of tropical colorful flowers, and a "Welcome Home Hadley" sign. Ouma totally made it, I could tell, but she gave Riaan the credit— it was cute. The reunion was spectacular. It had been about ten months since Riaan and I had seen each other last and almost twelve months since I had seen Ouma.

The following morning at 9:30 am we were to meet the Priest that would marry us the following day: Saturday, October 17th 2009. The three of us hopped into Ouma's vehicle chattering excitedly about the coming week-end. Riaan and I were finally getting married!

The next morning we woke up bright and early. Thanks to jet lag and excitement, I had only slept about three hours. The Priest came to Ouma's place for tea and biscuits, but to also discuss the following day's wedding ceremony schedule. The Priest was a small older gentleman who embraced us in big long hugs. He was warm and smelled like roses. He sat Riaan and myself down as well as Ouma and Riaan's Uncle, Rufus, to discuss the plan for the following day. He took us through a step-by-step detail of what the ceremony would entail, and helped us make some decisions on how everything would play out.

"Okay, people. We could do this one of two ways. One is you repeat after me, phrase by phrase. Or, I will speak out the vows in whole and you follow up with an I do." He air quoted the last two words. "Which one works better for you?"

"I am not good with my words. I think I would be more apt for just saying I do. What do you think Hadley my dear?" Riaan asked.

"I completely agree with you. I would probably get all flabbergasted and start to stutter." I said. I squeezed Riaan's hand, and then winked at him.

Once we finished our plans with the Priest, it was party time and getting to meet all Riaan's friends. This was a big deal since I had been out to South Africa over the span of three years, and I had only met a couple of his buddies. This group of people we were meeting that night was all of Riaan's high school buddies. There were six of them, and their girlfriends. The fourteen of us were going out to paint the town red.

Riaan and I walked into one of his friend's place to start the party. The house was full of people doing shots, snorting cocaine, and eating chips and dip as though it was totally normal. I had no idea what I was exactly getting into. People were passing the drugs and bottles of alcohol around. Every couple of minutes I had someone else asking me if I wanted something. I hadn't done any drugs since Riaan and I were last together, and it was never in a big group like this. I didn't know what to do.

"Let's have some fun tonight! We are getting married tomorrow. Let's blow off some steam." Riaan said. He grabbed my hand and gave me a kiss on the cheek.

So, Riaan and I popped some fun looking pills that turned everything into a fun love boat ride. We danced at a giant nightclub that was bigger than anything I have ever seen before. It held over 4,000 people, and it had seven DJ's spinning in different rooms. It was already mind blowing to begin with— let alone being high, the music moving the soul with the thumping and pounding. The flashing lights and sirens made me feel like I was in a dreamland. Once the night ended Riaan and I went home. Upon arriving home though, Riaan did the unthinkable.

It was truly an unforgettable moment.

He snuck into his Ouma's room and stole a small box. He then stripped down to absolutely nothing. He then knelt down on one knee with his penis flopping all over the place. He opened the little box he stole to show a beautiful white gold ring.

"Baby, I know I have asked you this before. I also know that you have already said yes, but I didn't have the opportunity to ask you properly in person. So please, will you do me the honor or marrying me in five hours? I can't wait to spend the rest of my life with you!"

"I am not going to lie your penis is extremely distracting right now!" I said, laughing. "I am having a hard time not staring. It almost looks like it is looking right at me! But yes, of course I will, and I can't wait!" I crawled on the bed to his kneeling naked body.

He stood up pulled the ring out of the box, and slid it on my finger. It was a bit big, but other than that, it was amazingly perfect

CHAPTER SEVEN

Wedding Vows

and Scorpions

When we finished up our shenanigans from the previous night, we only slept for about two hours. We hopped in the shower together, and giggled like little school kids the entire time. I put on a white sun dress that I had bought specially for the occasion, and Riaan put on a white dress shirt. We got dolled up and wedding ready. When we emerged into

Ouma's family room, she had put rose pedals and bunch of flowers all over the house. She had lit little tea lights all around the house, and it was a beautiful sight.

"Oh good morning you two love birds you. Did you get a good sleep last night? Ready for the big day?" Ouma asked. She hugged us tightly.

Riaan and I looked at each other giggled while nodding yes.

Shortly after the Priest showed up, Uncle Rufus arrived. They both embraced us tightly. They were both extremely emotional, in a positive way though, and it was very moving to see the joy this wedding brought the family.

"Let's get this party started," The Priest said as he pulled his papers out. He directed with his finger where Riaan and I had to stand. Both Uncle Rufus and Ouma followed and stood behind him to admire with their cameras ready for photos. "Let's begin!"

After some passages being read from the Bible, it was about time for the exchanging of our vows. My stomach started to ache and rumble. Last night's debauchery and substances started a tornado in my innards. I got lost in the consuming feeling of nausea. Riaan squeezed my hand to get my attention. He looked quizzically into my eyes when I glanced up. I nodded to let him know I was okay followed by a smile and a head shake. Last night was fun, but it was catching up to me, and I was about five minutes away from puking all over this Priest.

We got to "I do." I squeaked mine out quickly and in a giggle. I was so happy, and so anxious to get it over with. Upon Riaan's turn, it took him a moment to answer the Priest as he looked deep into my eyes. It felt as though he was staring at my soul, and it gave me a sense of comfort and serenity that I knew that was it. I knew that I had my prince charming.

"I do. I am so lucky." He said, not breaking his stare with me.

"You may kiss the bride now. Congratulations! I now pronounce you husband and wife." Before the Priest finished that sentence, Riaan grabbed my hands pulled me forward and embraced me in a long warm deep kiss. Ouma and Rufus applauded in the background between snapping photos.

After hugging everyone, and posing for a couple of photos, I excused myself to the bathroom. When I passed everyone, my pace quickened as I could feel the vomit crawl up the back of my throat. As soon as I closed the door behind me, I threw the tap on as high was it would go for background noise, and then kneeled over the toilet and hurled my guts out for the following five minutes. I barely ate the day before, and didn't eat that morning yet, but I was pretty sure that I vomited half of a cow. Once I finished upchucking every morsel in my stomach, I cleaned myself off and tried to touch up my makeup. I didn't want anyone to know what I had just done. It was embarrassing that I partied so hard the night before that I puked on my wedding day. I opened the bathroom door, and Riaan was standing right there.

"You okay babe?" He asked in concern, but chuckled a bit.

I threw my head into the palms of my hands. "I'm okay. Just a little too much last night I guess. I feel better now, though, thank goodness."

Once the hoopla of the ceremony was over, it was back to business. Riaan and I ensured

that the application for the marriage certificate was filled out correctly, and then followed the Priest to the specific office in town
where we needed to send it in and wait to ob-
tain the Marriage Certificate. He had warned
us that we needed to get it done that day so I
could take it home nine weeks later.

Shortly after we left, we arrived at this old
stinky building with a lineup of people out the
front door. Both Riaan and I looked at each
other in exhaustion since we had not slept the
night before, and now hundreds of people in a
line up. Luckily, the Priest walked us up and
through almost all the people. He introduced
us to a lady who took our information. She
asked for our contact information and then
told us we would be talking within the next 6
weeks or so.

South African's to go to time is always six
weeks. You will get your passport in six
weeks. You will get your Visa in six weeks.

You will get your Big Mac in six weeks. You know, no big deal for everything and anything. Just a six week deadline.

The following Thursday evening my parents, and brother flew in. On Friday, we introduced both sides of the family. Riaan's aunties, uncles, and cousins meshed amazingly with my family. Super loud and energetic people, shout outs of love and positivity, and they all loved their cocktails. When we threw in Riaan's parents, and sister, things then went awry.

They came in casual beach clothing and when they were dropped off by the bus, they were already half-loaded. Riaan's sister walked in with her lanky tall boyfriend. Both of them were pretty important in South Africa's underworld Goth parties from what Riaan told me. They were both extremely thin and covered head to toe in leather clothing with black and purple hair.

Needless to say, that dinner was a little bit awkward, but everyone made do. Riaan and I sat back and watched our families interact and have a great time celebrating our love. We both loved watching the happiness that brought our families to finally see us together, and living out our fairy tale.

Before we knew it the second wedding was upon us. We woke up very early on the Saturday morning, and everyone got their duties before heading straight to work. We had a couple of aunties and cousins putting out thousands of rose pedals throughout the yard, scattered across the pool, and also covering a makeshift aisle through the back yard. The caterer showed up and got all the tables, chairs, and tent set up. All the décor was a beautiful soft purple and dusty rose pink.

It looked like a fairy tale wedding, and all I had to do was show up in a wedding dress. With it being late spring, the weather was hot, humid, and sitting at a steady twenty-five degrees Celsius. My mum and I got all geared up to get me dressed. My damn body swelled from the heat, and the straps of my dress were sticking to my body until one ripped.

Hell, between the heat, and all the drinking and celebrating, it was a wonder I could even fit the dress over my hips. I had a hell of a time keeping everything in place, and tried not to make any sudden moves to avoid ripping another strap.

Then, the time came when all of Riaan's family, and friends started to show up. The party was about to begin. Beers were cracked open upon people's arrival, and the rugby game was on in the background. Both sides of the family were conversing and celebrating. It was great to see.

Riaan was a nervous wreck. He constantly ran around trying to find his parents, and made sure they were staying out of trouble. It seemed like every time he turned around someone was grabbing at him to deal with an issue. He was sweating through his suit within minutes of putting it on.

I found it kind of hot and sexy, actually. Hot, sweaty mess bundled up in a suit.

When the time came for the wedding to start, the beers were put aside, rugby shut off, and everyone congregated around the palapus where the priest and Riaan waited for me and my dad to walk down the aisle.

It was great to see so many faces standing there to celebrate this with us. Riaan and I had been so consumed with our situation and our struggle with Immigration that we forgot the impact that it had on the ones around us. I knew Riaan was happy and at peace. His eyes twinkled with excitement, and a small tear formed in the corner of his eye. My heart melted at that moment. I knew that we were on the right path.

It came to our vows, and this time around we had arranged to write our own vows, and exchange them. Riaan and I compared them to ensure that both of them were equally said. We were already legally married, but this was just another celebration in our eyes. Once it came to me saying mine, I completely forgot what I wrote, and started to ramble. Once the rambling started, the tears were there shortly after. After a couple of minutes of straight from the heart talk, I wrapped it up.

"Wow, well that was a bit unplanned. I love you too, baby" Riaan stammered out. He looked at me in confusion. I laughed, winked, and then squeezed his hands as an apology.

"Well, that's my wife for you. Always has the perfect thing to say! Thank you, my love. You said that so well that I have nothing to

say back to that. Well, except I will do whatever I have to do to become and stay your
prince charming. I will always love you until
the day I die, and I cannot wait to share the
remainder of my days with you." He looked up
at the Priest then. "Can I kiss her yet?"

Everyone in the congregation laughed
while some friends hooted and hollered in the
background. The Priest shook his head.
Riaan's parents insisted that they get the
Priest who married them almost thirty years
prior to marry us this time around. Even
though they didn't go to church, and hadn't
spoken to this man since their wedding, they
thought that it would be a delight. Ouma had
been appalled that they would even suggest
that since they married behind everyone's
back.

*This priest was dry and old and crusty and
couldn't take a joke while the bride and
groom were the most laid back people imagi-*

nable, and not religious. It was a terrible mix, but anything to keep the psycho mum happy. Right?!

After the ceremony was done, it was dinner time. Family and friends collected themselves plates full of food. As we were all sitting down we noticed that Pieter, Riaan's Best man, and one of the boys' girlfriend's were missing. We all knew that Pieter was a sweet talker on his good days, but to pick up another guy's girlfriend and date to our wedding was something that we didn't expect.

Riaan snuck out of the back of the tent to go wander around the yard to see whether he could find them. He found the both of them hunched over the sink going at it like wild dogs with a small mound of cocaine on the sink surface.

"Hey," Pieter slowed down his pumping. "Give us a minute?"

The girl winked at Riaan while bent over the counter top with her dress above her waist, panties around her knees, and a cocaine ring around her right nostril.

Riaan came back to tell me what he had just seen. While he finished the story, the girl's boyfriend, Harold, came up to us in a panic. "Yo, have you seen my chick? She's been missing for a bit."

"Um, I am sure she is fine, maybe check the parked cars?" Riaan shrugged his shoulder and pointed in the opposite direction of the bathroom where those two were going at it. We both looked at each other and shook our heads laughing— only at our wedding would this type of shit would happen.

As the night went on, we ate, drank, and danced. It was such a lovely time until about midnight. Riaan's mum was head banging on the dance floor to Louis Armstrong's, *What a*

Wonderful world. In my opinion, not a head banging type of song. But then, the head banging got worse, it turned into something anyone would expect to see on an acid trip. She started to shift her body into weird positions, and grab at imaginary things in the sky and in front of her. Then, the worst part of it all happened— she started to rub herself all over. It got so awkward that people stopped dancing around her, and eventually she was the only person left dancing.

Ouma was disgusted at the turn of events, and tried to stop her. Riaan's mum spun out of reach of Ouma and dipped away only to suddenly fling her entire body towards Ouma unexpectedly, and took Ouma out. Poor Ouma went flying, and banged her head on the hard cement ground. Riaan's mum didn't notice and kept on going while enjoying the acid trip wave she was experiencing.

The entire party of people stopped and attended to Ouma. She was fine, luckily. We gave her an ice pack and a wine spritzer and continued on with our night. Riaan was mortified that his mother would act that way. Even my own parents were more attentive to Ouma than her own daughter.

The party ended shortly after Ouma's fall. Riaan and I walked down the street back to Ouma's place where we were staying. Exhausted and half-drunk, we stumbled back and forth across the street reminiscing about all the wonderful and hilariously random things that happened that day.

Second wedding was officially a success.

We had a day recovery before we as a McLeary family went on a four day safari. My parents and brother took Riaan and I out of town for our first family trip. We drove four hours north into the mountains and through deep valleys until we hit the safari camps. We did four days of true South African tourism. We first experienced a nighttime safari where we drove through the camp as the sunset, which meant that it would cool off and the animals would emerge again, getting ready to feed.

As a celebration, my brother, myself, and Riaan decided to have a couple of cocktails prior to departing on the three-hour venture. That was the worst idea ever since there aren't any bathrooms in the bush. There was only a bush in the bush. On top of that, the bushes were full of meat eating animals, poisonous bugs, and reptiles. About an hour into the ride, my bladder was ready to explode, and the boys were contemplating about just wizzing over the side of the truck. Totally one-hundred percent unfair to me.

Jerks.

The guide pulled off to the side, and took a pee for himself. The three of us took the opportunity to hop off the truck and squat. Well, I squatted off the side of the truck; and terrified of the Rhinos that were drinking water less than one-hundred yards away- with one hand keeping my undies from getting peed on, and the other knuckling the truck bumper.

After everyone relieved themselves, we hit the road again. Throughout our trek we spotted a lion that had just finished feeding, a cheetah and her two cubs playing in a field, and a whole slew of bucks and zebras. It was amazing, and even Riaan was amazed. He said that it was rare to see all the animals that we saw, and it was only day one of the safari.

The remainder of the safari was as successful as our first night ride. We woke up the last morning to take a ride on the elephants through the savannah. We had to get up at

4:30 am in order to get to the park where the elephants were, and get on them before it got too hot. It was the most relaxing and most peaceful time of the four days. We were jam packed full of activities and plans that we didn't have any down time. Upon getting on the elephants, their slow methodical moves almost rocked me to sleep. I didn't want it to end.

On the last night of our trip, we were all in our own rooms getting ready for our dinner. It was the one time of day that was quiet and peaceful when a loud shriek echoed in the distance.

"Shit! That sounded like Blake!" I said. I waited to see if anything else happened after the noise.

"Riaan!" "Riiiaaaaaannn" we heard in the distance followed by stomping.

"Here he comes,"` Riaan giggled. He walked to the door to meet a panicked, and half-naked Blake.

"There is a scorpion in my bathroom, and I almost died. I need to get out of fucking Africa. It interrupted my shower. I tried to put it in a cup, and grabbed a towel then ran here. Help me," he said, pleadingly.

We gathered ourselves and gave Blake a bigger towel to cover himself with as we walked to his room. My parents joined us on the walk through the camp. Blake waved his hand in front of his face trying to cool himself off. From an outsider's perspective, it was really hard not to laugh. He was genuinely freaked out.

We got to his room, and Riaan picked up the cup that Blake placed over the scorpion.

"Oh, yeah, this little guy is a nasty one. Good thing you got it with the cup. I'll set it outside, and everything will be all right." Riaan said. He carefully scooped it up with a piece of paper and the cup.

"Fuck that! Kill it now!" Blake swatted at the cup while hopping on his tippy toes.

"No we can't. This guy will be fine once we put him outside. I will put him far away from your cabin so he won't bother you." Riaan said, shielding Blake's attempt at swatting the cup. He didn't like to kill things. He had a conservative mentality and liked to preserve wildlife as much as possible. It was a joy to watch him, although it was even more of a joy to watch my baby brother freak out over this.

I am well aware that I am an evil big sister.

The family trip ended well. It was great getting to spend time with my parents and brother and husband all in the same area for once. Everyone seemed to get along really well, and seemed happy— minus my poor brother. The wild didn't sit well with him, and he preferred the concrete jungle with designer suits, high-end vehicles, and Grey Goose Vodka. He survived well though, and we were all really proud of him at the end of the trip.

My three months in South Africa flew by, and before we knew it I was on the plane home, wedding certificate in hand, and all the important documents ready to go. I arrived home mid-December, ready for Christmas, and ready to get a job and start prepping for Riaan to finally come home, to our home.

It took us five months to get all supporting documents in line. We compiled a 167 page application, proving the authenticity of our love and relationship, disproving Riaan's criminal past – with help from my mum, and compiling all the emails, love letters, and photos of our four years of long distance romance. By mid-May, I sent the application into the Immigration office. Riaan and I started to pray for great news.

Thirty days passed when I got my notice of acceptance for a sponsor. It was the happiest day ever, and I called Riaan in tears of joy. First part down, and then the hard part followed. Now, it was time where the Canadian Immigration would assess Riaan as a person to see if he would be an asset to our society. Months and months passed. We were nearing about nine months at one point. Riaan and I had been apart for thirteen months, and it was the longest we had been apart ever. We had spent the first year of marriage over 5,000 kilometers a part from each other. We were better than ever though.

I had found a great job as an event coordinator. I was planning weddings, and surrounded by love all of the time. It helped me stay positive about my marriage. Finally one day, about ten months into the application for Riaan, he got the letter in the mail. Accepted!

The day had finally come, Riaan called me so excited he was nearly speechless. "I never thought this day would come," he said, stuttering in excitement. "I can't believe it is finally here."

"When are you coming home?" That was all I kept asking. I wanted him to pack his bags and leave the next day.

We both were numb with excitement. In the back of our minds, we were both shit scared of the reality of what was about to happen. Riaan more so than me. He was the one who was packing up his life in his home country, and coming to live here without his family. Over the past four years, we had only dreamt of and talked about living in Canada. It had never become a reality because of all the bad news we continued to receive from Canadian Immigration. After a couple of days, the numbness wore off and Riaan started to plan his journey to Canada.

As excited as we both were to finally to have our happily ever after, we both had no idea what lay ahead of us, and what was to come next.

ABOUT THE AUTHOR

Amongst her friends and family, Miranda Oh is known
to be the storyteller of the group, always recapping
crazy life stories and situations. When not playing the
corporate part she can be found sipping wine and
spending all her hard-earned money on shoes.
'Remember, No Matter What: Chin Up, Tits Out" is
the first of many novels you'll be seeing from Miranda
Oh.

I would love to connect with you:
www.ohmirandaoh.com
www.facebook.com/ohmirandaoh
www.twitter.com/ohmirandaoh
www.amazon.com/author/ohmirandaoh